Otter *and* Odder

James Howe

illustrated by **Chris Raschka**

CANDLEWICK PRESS

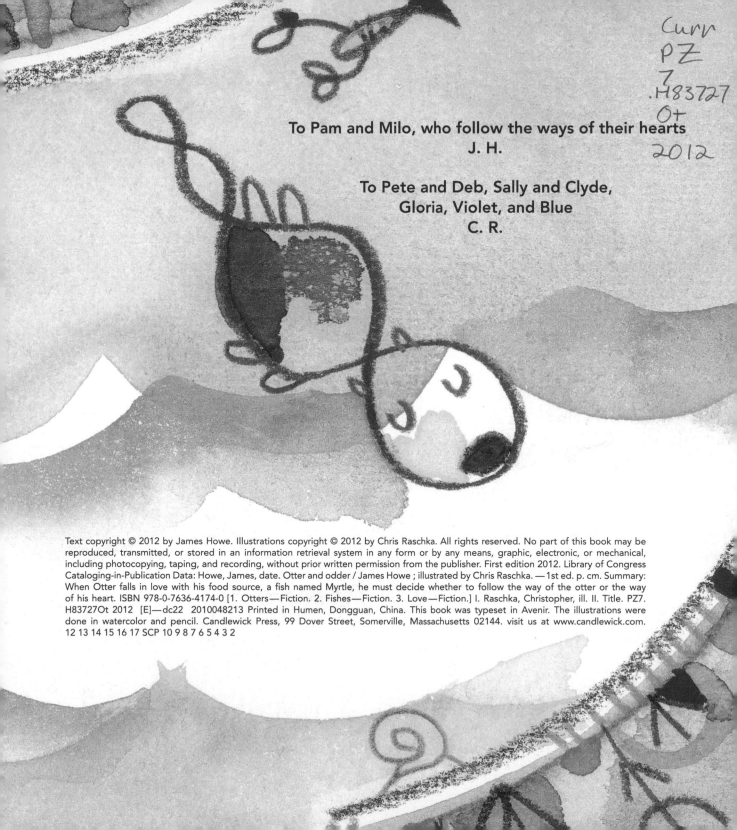

To Pam and Milo, who follow the ways of their hearts
J. H.

To Pete and Deb, Sally and Clyde,
Gloria, Violet, and Blue
C. R.

The river sparkled
the day Otter found love.
He was not looking for it
(love, that is).
He was looking for dinner.

But when Otter gazed into those eyes—
those round, sweet, glistening eyes—
he knew that he had found what he had
not known he was looking for.
"Impossible," he said.
"I am in love with my food source."

He asked her name
(not certain if she was a he
or he was a she;
something about the eyes
told him *she*).

She said, "Gurgle."
But because he had water in his ears,
Otter heard it as *Myrtle*
and thought,
*Such a beautiful name to match
such beautiful eyes.*

And so it was that Otter fell in love
with a fish.

Myrtle (or Gurgle, if you prefer)
had not been looking for love, either.
She had been looking to stay alive.
Please don't eat me,
her round, sweet, glistening eyes
pleaded with Otter
while he was gazing into them,
finding love.

All she wanted was a loosening of his grip,
a slippery escape,
a return to the safety of family and home.
But then in his eyes
she saw the sparkling river reflected
and a tender and lonely heart revealed.
And the stirrings of her own
heart—
her own tremulous
fish-not-wishing-to-be-dinner
heart—
awakened to something
new and surprising:
not only love but a future
she could never have imagined.

From that moment on,
Otter and Myrtle were rarely apart.
They swam together.
They played hide-and-go-seek together.
They told each other stories—
hers of the depths of the river,
his of the banks and beyond.
They warmed their faces in the morning sun

and silently considered the stars that filled
the midnight sky.

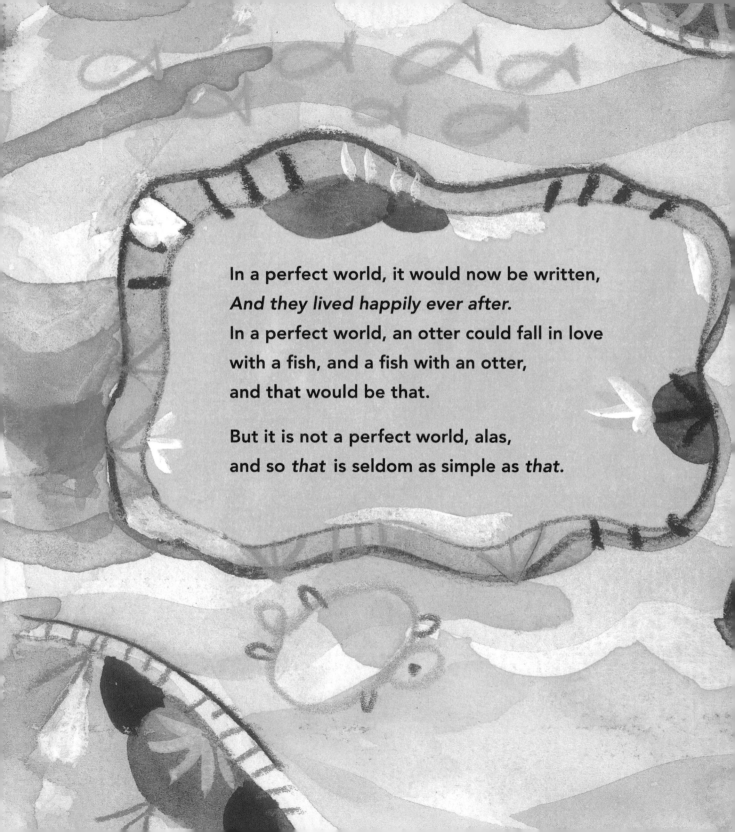

In a perfect world, it would now be written,
And they lived happily ever after.
In a perfect world, an otter could fall in love
with a fish, and a fish with an otter,
and that would be that.

But it is not a perfect world, alas,
and so *that* is seldom as simple as *that*.

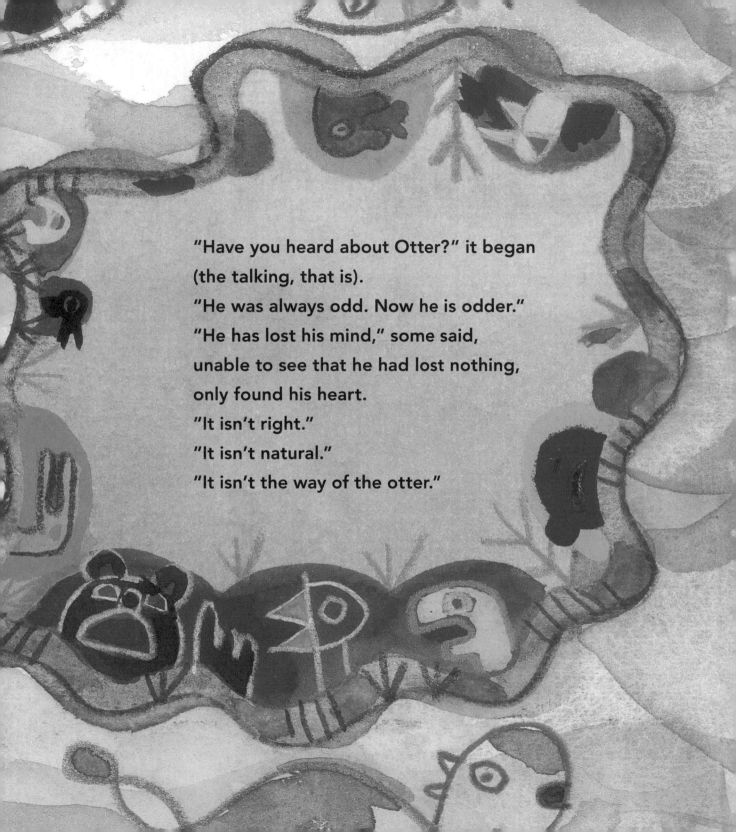

"Have you heard about Otter?" it began
(the talking, that is).
"He was always odd. Now he is odder."
"He has lost his mind," some said,
unable to see that he had lost nothing,
only found his heart.
"It isn't right."
"It isn't natural."
"It isn't the way of the otter."

Day after day,
night after night,
Otter heard the talk
and wondered:
What is right? What is wrong?
What is natural?
What is the way of the otter?

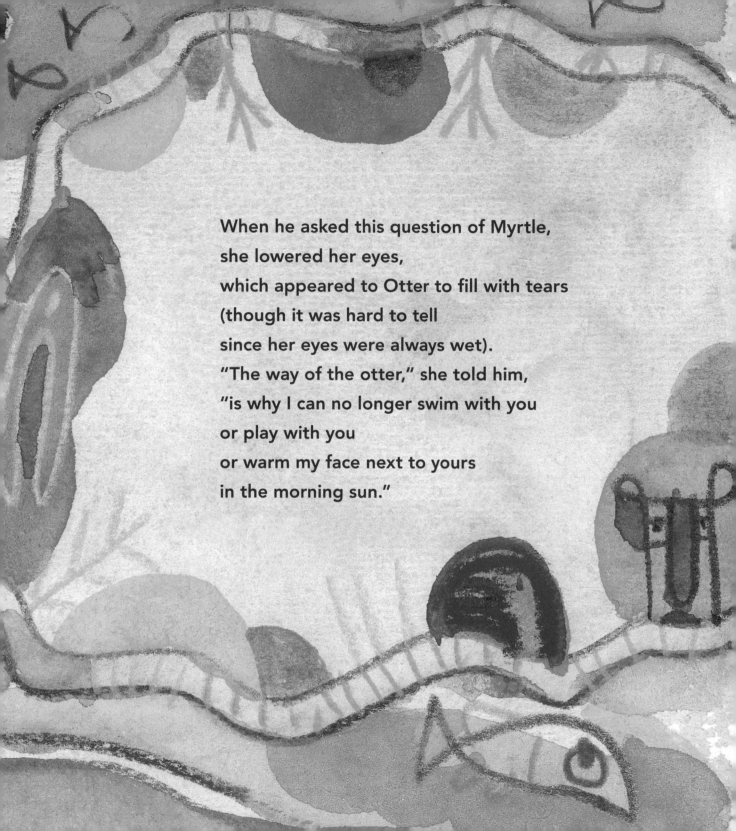

When he asked this question of Myrtle,
she lowered her eyes,
which appeared to Otter to fill with tears
(though it was hard to tell
since her eyes were always wet).
"The way of the otter," she told him,
"is why I can no longer swim with you
or play with you
or warm my face next to yours
in the morning sun."

A reed, standing close, leaned into Otter
as if to be sure he was still breathing.
"Do you no longer love me?" Otter asked,
his voice little more than a whisper.
"I am no longer sure a fish *can* love an otter,"
Myrtle replied, "when the way of the otter
is to eat fish."

Now Otter's eyes grew wet with tears.

"I must eat," he said.

"But must you eat my friends?" Myrtle asked.

"My family?"

Otter had no answer.

Feeling an old loneliness return,

he watched Myrtle swim away.

In a tragic tale, it would now be written,
And so their love could never be.
In a tragic tale, an otter could never love
a fish, nor a fish love an otter,
and that would be that.

But this is not a tragic tale.
It contains hope.
And so the ending is yet to be written.

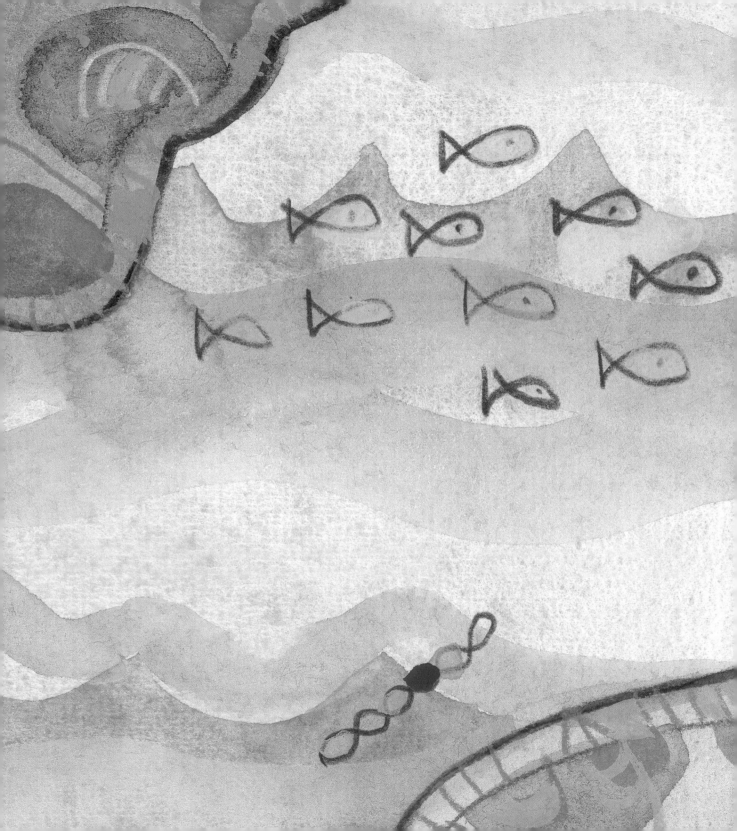

"Otter has come to his senses," it began
(the talking, that is).
"Now he will forget all about this
falling-in-love-with-fish nonsense," some said,
unable to know that falling in love is never
nonsense.
Otter tried not to listen,
but in time he thought,
They're right.
It is impossible.
You cannot love your food source.

But when he warmed his face
in the morning sun,
he imagined Myrtle beside him.
And when he gazed at the midnight sky,
he saw Myrtle's eyes a thousandfold.
*Is it the way of the otter, he wondered,
to be alone?*

One morning Otter floated his way
to Beaver's house.
"Good morning," Beaver called out.
"Care for a bit of birch bark?"
Otter wrinkled his nose.
"Otters don't eat bark," he said,
"but thank you for your kindness."
"Ah," said Beaver.
"How about an apple then?"
Otter shook his head.

"Apples are awfully tasty,"
Beaver went on. "Tastier, I find,
than fish."
Otter pulled himself up onto a log
to look Beaver in the eye.
"Have you ever eaten fish?" Otter asked.
"No," said Beaver, "but I suppose I might
if I ever fell in love with
an apple."

Beaver was known for his wisdom,
and in that moment Otter knew he had found the wisdom
he had not known he was looking for.
"Are you saying . . . " Otter began.
"I am saying," said Beaver, "that there is
the way of the otter
and there is
the way of the heart.
It is up to you to decide which to follow."

Otter ate a bite of the apple, a bite of the bark,
and the fruit of a water lily, which he found
to be especially delicious.
"Thank you," said Otter.
"You're welcome," said Beaver. "And next time,
bring Myrtle. There's some lovely plankton
just on the other side of the dam."

That night Otter was considering the stars when he heard
a familiar *splish*.

"Beaver told me I would find you here," Myrtle said as
she swam up to him. "My family was wondering if you
would come play with us tomorrow."

"I would love to," said Otter. "Perhaps we could have dinner
together. Have you ever eaten the bark of the aspen tree?"

"I could try it," Myrtle said.

"It's quite tasty," said Otter. "Much tastier than fish.
I don't know what I ever saw in fish."

Myrtle wriggled against Otter's side.

"Except for you, dear Myrtle," he said. "Except for you."

It wasn't long before the talking began again.

"It isn't right."

"It isn't natural."

"It isn't the way of the otter."

But Otter and Myrtle did not listen.

They swam together.

They played hide-and-go-seek together.

They discussed the mysteries of life and love
with Beaver while dining on plankton
and apples and the fruit of the water lily.
They warmed their faces in the morning sun
and silently considered the stars that filled the midnight sky.

And now it can be written . . .

And they lived happily ever after.